THE
SUMMER VACATION
FROM THE
BLACK LAGOON®

Have a great summer!

♡ Mrs. McKeown

I'VE READ THEM ALL.

Get more monster-sized laughs from

The Black Lagoon®

THE
SUMMER VACATION
FROM THE
BLACK LAGOON®

by Mike Thaler
Illustrated by Jared Lee

SCHOLASTIC INC.

New York Toronto London Auckland
Sydney Mexico City New Delhi Hong Kong

To Alex & Betty Wagner
for bringing up Patty so well.
—M.T.

To Jody Greer.
—J.L.

ISBN 978-0-545-07224-3

Text copyright © 2010 by Mike Thaler
Illustrations copyright © 2010 by Jared D. Lee Studio, Inc.

All rights reserved. Published by Scholastic Inc.

SCHOLASTIC, LITTLE APPLE, and associated logos are trademarks and/or registered trademarks of Scholastic Inc. BLACK LAGOON is a registered trademark of Mike Thaler and Jared D. Lee Studio, Inc. All rights reserved. Lexile is a registered trademark of MetaMetrics, Inc.

12 11 10 9 8 7 6   10 11 12 13 14 15/0

Printed in the U.S.A.   40
First printing, May 2010

CONTENTS

BACK →

← FRONT

CHAPTER 1
SUMMER BUMMER

Well, it's the first day of summer vacation. It is going to be the longest day of the year. I lie in bed thinking about what to do.

Should I go right back to sleep? Should I get up?

Should I brush my teeth, my hair, or my dog?

Should I clean my hands, my face, or my room?

All of my friends are at camp. Eric went to baseball camp with Derek. Freddy went to chef camp, Randy went to space camp, Doris went to dance camp, and Penny is in boot camp. They all have plenty to do, and many to do it with.

I'm all alone, I'm bored, and it's only the first day of summer.

I think I'll go back to sleep.

RANDY →

WE HAVE A BLASTOFF, HOUSTON.

CHAPTER 2
SUMMER DREAM

I'm crossing a very big desert. I wish I had another "s"—then it would be a *dessert*.

THIS ISN'T SO BAD.

9

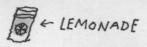 ← LEMONADE

There are no signs, so I don't know where I am, or where I'm going. Actually, it doesn't matter; it's the same in every direction— lots of sand, space, and sun. I wish I had a big lemonade and a little shade. Maybe my own parade. I'd still be hot . . . but I wouldn't be alone.

CHAPTER 3
TIME ON MY HANDS

I wake up again. It's only eight o'clock. I could get up and brush my teeth. That won't take all day. I could go have breakfast, *then* brush my teeth.

12

I think I need a more significant project. I could make something: a car, a boat, a plane, a mess.

I could build the model I got for Christmas. But I think I lost some of the parts.

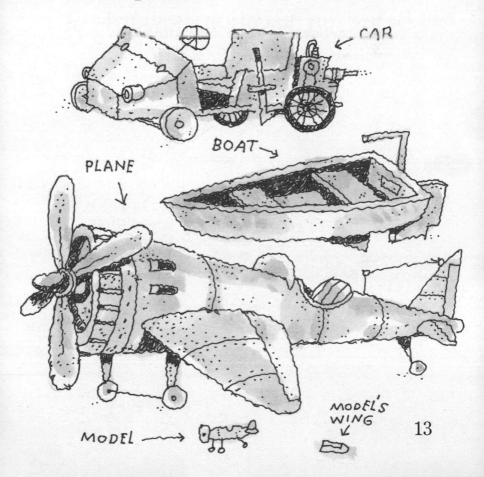

CAR

BOAT

PLANE

MODEL →

MODEL'S WING

 ← DIARY

I could exercise. I think I have all of the parts—arms, legs, and feet.

I could keep a diary, but then I still have to think of something to do so I can write about it.

Being on vacation is hard—it was easier going to school.

CHAPTER 4
CHORES

I go ask Mom for something to do. Big mistake!

She has *lots* for me to do. Clean my room, wash the dog, wax the car, take out the trash, mow the lawn, etc., etc., etc.

Come on, Mom—this is my vacation!

Besides, I'm busy trying to think of something to do. Wow, that was close.

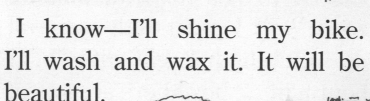

CHAPTER 5
THERE'S NO PLACE LIKE FOAM

I know—I'll shine my bike. I'll wash and wax it. It will be beautiful.

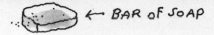

I fill a bucket with water and look for soap. Mom's got all kinds of soap: dish soap, laundry soap, face soap, bath soap, but no bike soap. Well, I guess bath soap will do—they both begin with "b." I pour it in . . . boy, there are lots of bubbles! Uh-oh, it's foaming out of the bucket.

AMAZED

FOAM

HOSE

BUCKET

19

I've created the bubble monster from the Black Lagoon. Well, now I have *one* thing to write in my diary.

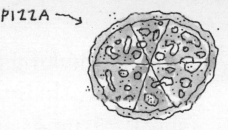
PIZZA →

CHAPTER 6
ODD JOBS

I guess I could get a summer job.

But *summer* better than others.

I could be a lifeguard . . . but I can't swim.

I could deliver pizzas . . . but I don't drive.

DON'T GO OUT TOO FAR, I CAN'T SWIM.

I CAN'T, EITHER.

NOR I.

I could be an astronaut . . . but I'm afraid of heights. I have a very short résumé and no degree, even though it's very hot today.

My only skills are picking my nose and crossing my eyes. These are not big in the job market.

CHAPTER 7
IF LIFE HANDS YOU LEMONS, MAKE LEMONADE

I could go into business for myself and become a captain of industry.

Let's see . . . I could cut lawns—nope—too hot; wash cars—I've got the bubbles; open a lemonade stand—you've got to stand for something.

That's it! I'll start with one stand—then open another, and another, and another. I'll have an empire! I'll be Julius Squeezer, the lemon king.

27

CHAPTER 8
A SWEET SPOT

What do I need for my stand? Lemons. Yes, I'll need lemons for sure.

I ask Mom if she has any. She points to her car.

"No, Mom—the fruit kind."

She looks in the fridge. In the very back of the fruit bin are two shriveled lemons. They look like little shrunken heads. Well, it's a start.

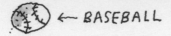 ← BASEBALL

I get a pitcher (not a catcher) and squeeze the lemons. Then I add water. Lots of water. Mom says to put in some sugar. So I pour in a whole bag.

Then I stir it all up. Time to taste it. I pour a little in Tailspin's bowl.

← CATCHER

He comes over, sniffs it, and walks away.

Everyone's a critic. I guess it needs more sugar. I pour in another bag. When I try to stir it, the spoon sticks. It's almost solid now. Maybe I should make Popsicles instead.

CORN DOG →

A SMALL TREE →

WELL?

NO COMMENT.

CHAPTER 9
OPEN FOR BUSINESS

Well I'm in business—almost. I get a box and make a sign: POPSICLES 25¢. I put it on the sidewalk in front of my house, get a folding chair, and I'm in business. All I need now are customers. It's a little slow this morning. Nobody's out on the street. Maybe the whole neighborhood has gone to camp. Maybe I should move my location.

Location is everything. I relocate to the corner. Now I've got four streets. Four empty streets. Where is everyone?

I've also got eight Popsicles that are beginning to sweat. I'm beginning to sweat, too. Business is harder than I thought. I change the sign.

There's not a rush. A garbage truck drives by. Mr. Debris, the garbage man, waves as he turns the corner.

The sun is hot. The Popsicles are wet. I change the sign.

POPSICLES 15¢

One car drives by.

The Popsicles are melting.

POPSICLES 5¢

They're dissolving.

They're puddles . . . victims of global warming.

I change the sign.

LEMONADE 25¢

CHAPTER 10
MIND OVER MATTER

Well, so much for business. I know what I'll do—I'll get a book and improve my mind.

LOOKS STICKY.

I close shop and clean up. It's not a toxic waste site, but it's very sticky. I get on my bright bike and pedal to the library. Uh-oh—it's closed. There's a sign on the door. I hope it doesn't say LEMONADE 5¢. No, it says SUMMER HOURS – CLOSED MONDAY. Today is Monday.

DRAT!

LIBRARY

CLOSED

The first day of summer vacation.

Eight weeks to go. I hate summer.

WHO ARE YOU?

GOURD →

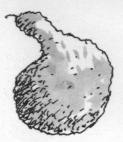

CHAPTER 11
BORED OUT OF MY GOURD

Well, I'm back to square one.
It's a big square.
An empty square.
A square square.

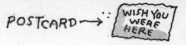
I go back to my room and lie down. I guess I'm on rectangle one. I need to think. Ideas just aren't coming. My mind has gone on vacation, too. Maybe it's at camp. I hope it's having a good time.

I hope it sends me a postcard with an idea on it.

HUBIE'S BRAIN →

CHAPTER 12

CALL OF THE WILD

The phone rings. Maybe it's my mind calling.

"Hello?"

"Who's this?"

"Hubie."

GLADYS ←

"Hubie who?"

"Hubie cool."

"Is Gladys there?"

"Gladys who?"

"Gladys Pinbottom."

RING!

GLADYS?

"No, I think you have the wrong number."

"If I got the wrong number, why did you answer the phone?" *Click!*

You know, this just proves that however bad things are, they can always get worse.

CHAPTER 13
TIME-OUT

I think I'll take a nap. A summer nap. A siesta.

At school you can't take naps, unless you're sick and go to the nurse's office. But the bed in there

←HARD AS A ROCK

is too hard. It's more like a board. I guess that's what they mean by room and board. And the pillow— forget it. It's a pill that is too hard to swallow.

Well, my bed is soft and my pillow is fluffy. I guess life's not so bad after all.

45

CHAPTER 14
A FLIGHTMARE

During my nap I have a dream. I'm in a rocket ship. It looks like a lemon. It *is* a lemon.

I guess I'm an astronaut, or a *lemonaut*.

Anyway, we're headed straight
for the sun. My lemon is melting.
It's getting smaller and smaller.

REALLY,
REALLY
HOT

DO NOT
TOUCH

It's gone and I'm falling through space. I land in my room, right on my own bed. I wake up. Well, here I am—maybe it really happened.

I know what I'll do—I'll write a story about my summer vacation.

← STILL ASLEEP

CHORES

← FULLY AWAKE

I'll get some paper and a pencil, so at least there'll be a record in case I die of boredom.

CHAPTER 15
THAT'S CALL, FOLKS

I sharpen my pencil and stack my paper in a neat pile.

Let's see—how do I start? Where do I start? Starting is always hard. I check my eraser—it works.

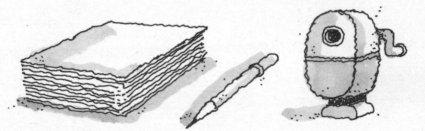

I sharpen my pencil again.

I straighten my paper again—I'm ready to start writing. Suddenly the phone rings. Oh joy, saved by the bell.

51

GLADYS UPSET →

"Hello?"
"Hello. Who's this?"
"Hubie."
"Hubie who?"
"Hubie cool. Who's this?"
"Gladys."
"Gladys who?"
"Gladys Pinbottom. Any messages?"
Click!

GLADYS, I'M TRYING TO WRITE.

CLICK!

DID YOU KNOCK?

CHAPTER 16
WAITING ON A LINE

☼ ← TINY SUN

Life is strange.

Back to the drawing board—or the writing desk, to finish my masterpiece. Well, actually, to start it. Let's see . . . where was I, where am I, where do I want to go?

☼

TINY BUG →

IDEA

THINKING CAP

HMMMM...

"It was the best of summers, it was the worst of summers. . . ."

I read that beginning line somewhere. I think it was *A Tale of Two Cities*—Cleveland and Cincinnati.

I could borrow the line. Sort of like recycling . . . but more like stealing. Well, my eraser works. I'm back to square one again. I guess my ethics didn't go to camp.

CHAPTER 17
A-MUSING

I'm getting pretty familiar with square one. I just may spend my whole summer in it. Wait! I have an idea.

← ANOTHER IDEA

← SQUARE ONE

REMEMBER GLADYS? →

"Once upon a time . . ." That's a good beginning. All the fairy tales begin that way. I guess they don't mind recycling. It's not stealing, but it's not original, either. I want my story to be original, 'cause I'm an original kind of guy.

Besides, my story is not a fairy tale—it's more like a nightmare.

CHAPTER 18
ON MY WAY!

I sharpen my pencil again. The point wore down a little. Now it is nice and sharp. I clean my eraser. I straighten my paper . . . I'm ready to roll. I can see it now: I write a hit story, a classic. I sell the movie rights, I go to Hollywood openings, I meet lots of stars, I win awards, I get an A in English. All I have to do is start it. Let's see . . . "Well, it's summer vacation . . ."

That's good—straightforward, honest—I like it.

CLAP!
CLAP!
CLAP!

THANKS, ANGELA.

It's a good beginning. Then the phone rings. I answer.

"Gladys isn't here—you've got the wrong number!"

"Hubie?"

"Yes, who's this?"

"Eric!"

"Eric who?"

"Eric, your best friend."

"I thought you were at camp."

"It doesn't start till next week. What are you doing?"

"I'm writing a story about summer vacation."

"Are you busy?"

"Nope."

"Do you want to ride our bikes to the park and play, then go to the movies, then sleep over at my house . . . Hubie, are you there?"

"No! I'm on my way to your house!"

EPILOGUE

Well, I had a great summer. When the library opened, I joined the summer reading program. I read lots of great books.

Eric's camp was only two weeks long and when he came back he showed me a lot of cool baseball stuff.

TRY AND HIT MY SINKER.

WOW!

STRIKE THREE!

WHAT A PITCH!

Then, the rest of the kids got back and we put on a magic show and a play.

Mom took us all to the museum and the water park.

It turned out to be the best summer I ever had, and I even found time to write this story.
I hope you like it.